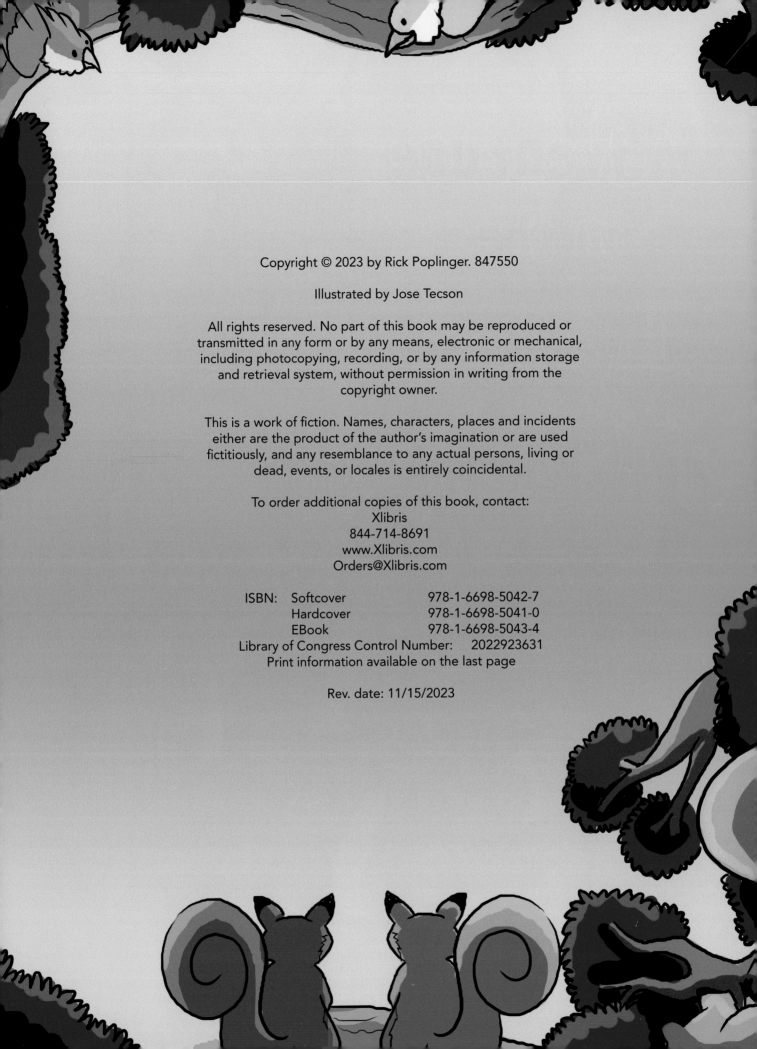

To order additional copies of this book, contact:
Xlibris
844-714-8691
www.Xlibris.com
Orders@Xlibris.com

ISBN: Softcover   978-1-6698-5042-7
         Hardcover   978-1-6698-5041-0
         EBook   978-1-6698-5043-4
Library of Congress Control Number: 2022923631
Print information available on the last page

Rev. date: 11/15/2023

My trilogy, **"Adventures in the Land of Changes"**, is dedicated to my two sons, Eitan and Gilad Poplinger.

Hey guys! Have I ever told you how happy I'm your father?

Book 1: **"The Ever-Changing Forest"**, is dedicated to my niece, Katie Schwamb

Book 2: **"The Ever-Changing Water"**, is dedicated to my niece, Courtney Schwamb

Book 3: **"The Ever-Changing Sky"**, is dedicated to my niece, Becca Poplinger

The Ever-Changing Forest

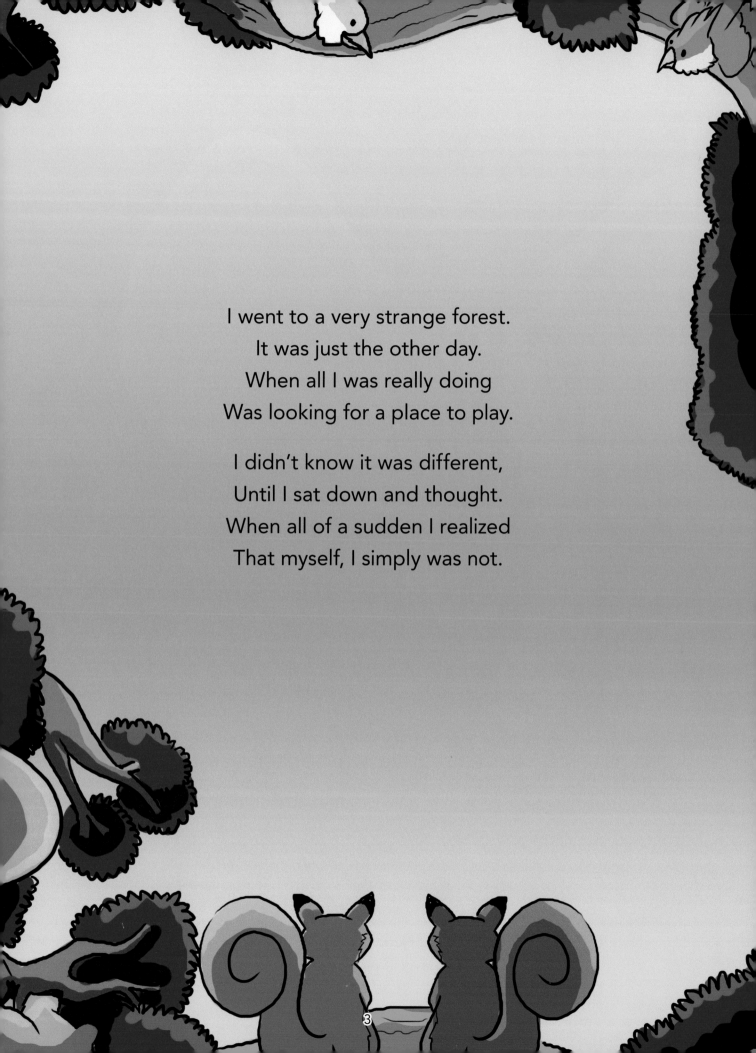

I went to a very strange forest.
It was just the other day.
When all I was really doing
Was looking for a place to play.

I didn't know it was different,
Until I sat down and thought.
When all of a sudden I realized
That myself, I simply was not.

4

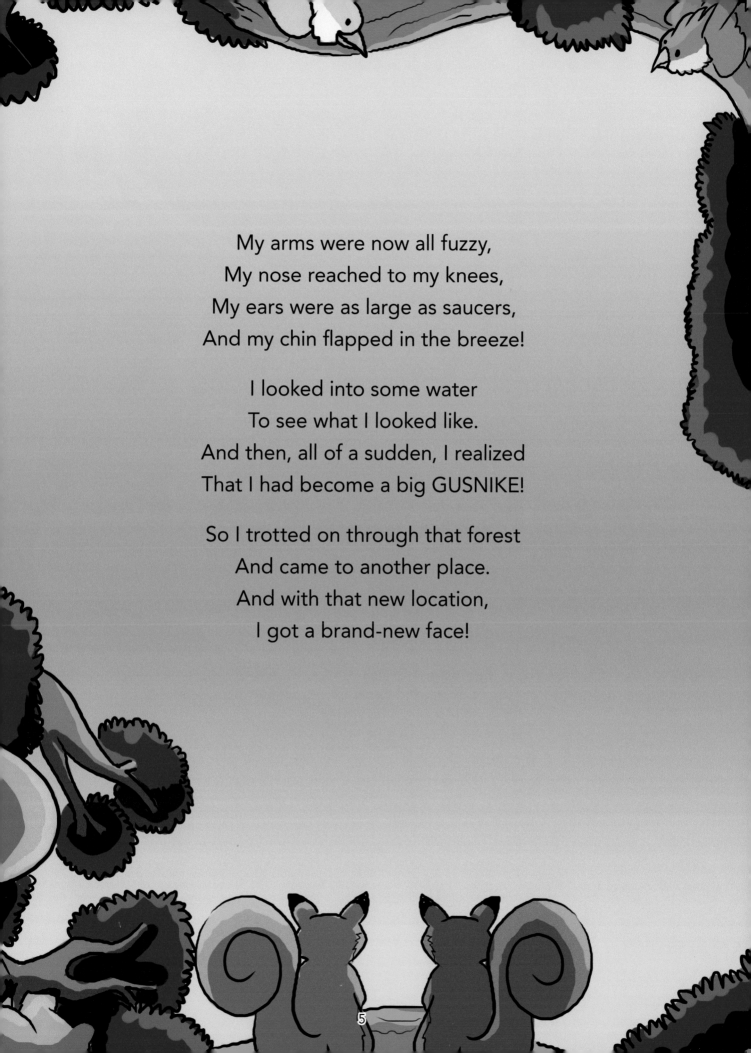

My arms were now all fuzzy,
My nose reached to my knees,
My ears were as large as saucers,
And my chin flapped in the breeze!

I looked into some water
To see what I looked like.
And then, all of a sudden, I realized
That I had become a big GUSNIKE!

So I trotted on through that forest
And came to another place.
And with that new location,
I got a brand-new face!

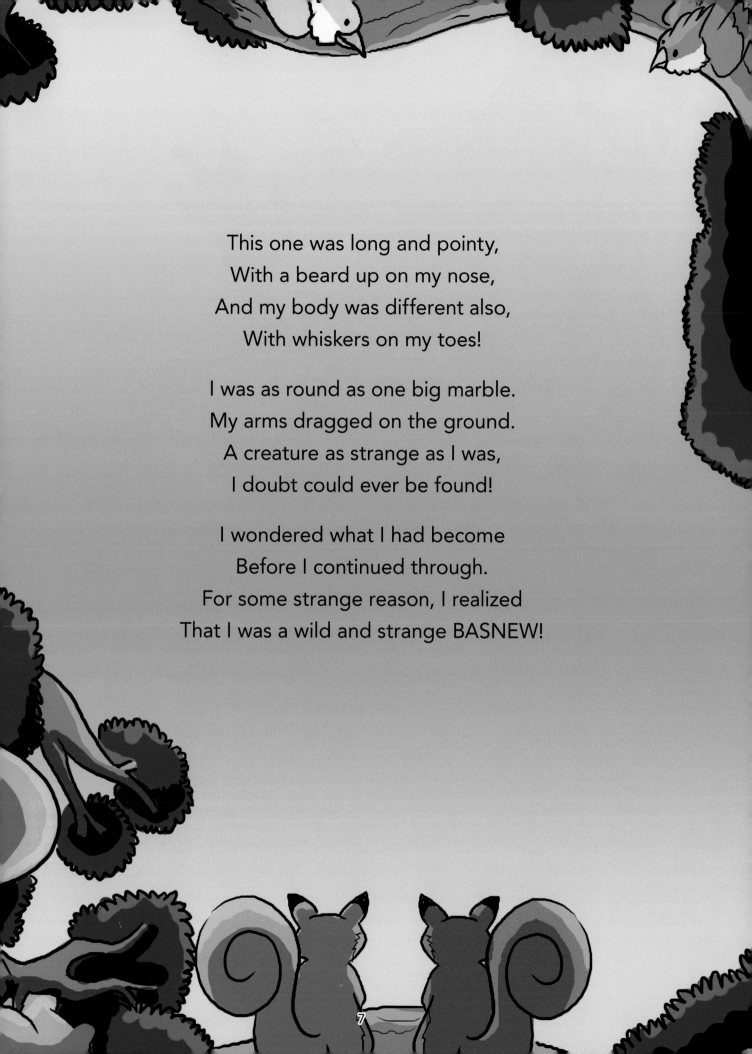

This one was long and pointy,
With a beard up on my nose,
And my body was different also,
With whiskers on my toes!

I was as round as one big marble.
My arms dragged on the ground.
A creature as strange as I was,
I doubt could ever be found!

I wondered what I had become
Before I continued through.
For some strange reason, I realized
That I was a wild and strange BASNEW!

Then I came up to some water
And sat upon a log,
Till I fell into the pond so clear
And became a WOLLY JOG!

My body was long and narrow.
My head was greatly bloated.
I began to swim around quite fast,
But on the top, I only floated.

I had ten feet with blue toenails
And eyelids of pink and green.
I did the backstroke while swimming.
I was a sight you never have seen!

So I swam up to the very top,
On to the water's edge.
I wanted to be just something else,
So I got up on the ledge!

And then I began just walking,
Just like a normal guy.
But I flapped my arms a little,
And suddenly, I began to fly!

My arms had turned to feathers.
My feet formed one great tail!
I had a propeller on my top notch,
Which made me fly and sail!

Then, finally, it just occurred to me
That a HELIOKLUNK I was.
I was covered with all these feathers.
Except on my face, there was only fuzz.

So I flew down into the forest,
Till I landed on a tree.
And I felt myself start changing,
And I wondered what I'd be.

Then I noticed that I was swinging
From that branch to another tree.
I had turned into a hairy beast.
I was called a green GLUNKEY!

With two tails on my backside
And a snout like a big fat pig,
I could land upon the biggest branch
Or upon the smallest twig.

I had arms without any elbows
And legs that had no knees.
I had a tongue that licked my eyebrows,
And I itched from all those fleas!

It was just too much; I had to change.
I was the strangest one around.
I knew I had to be different,
So I jumped down to the ground!

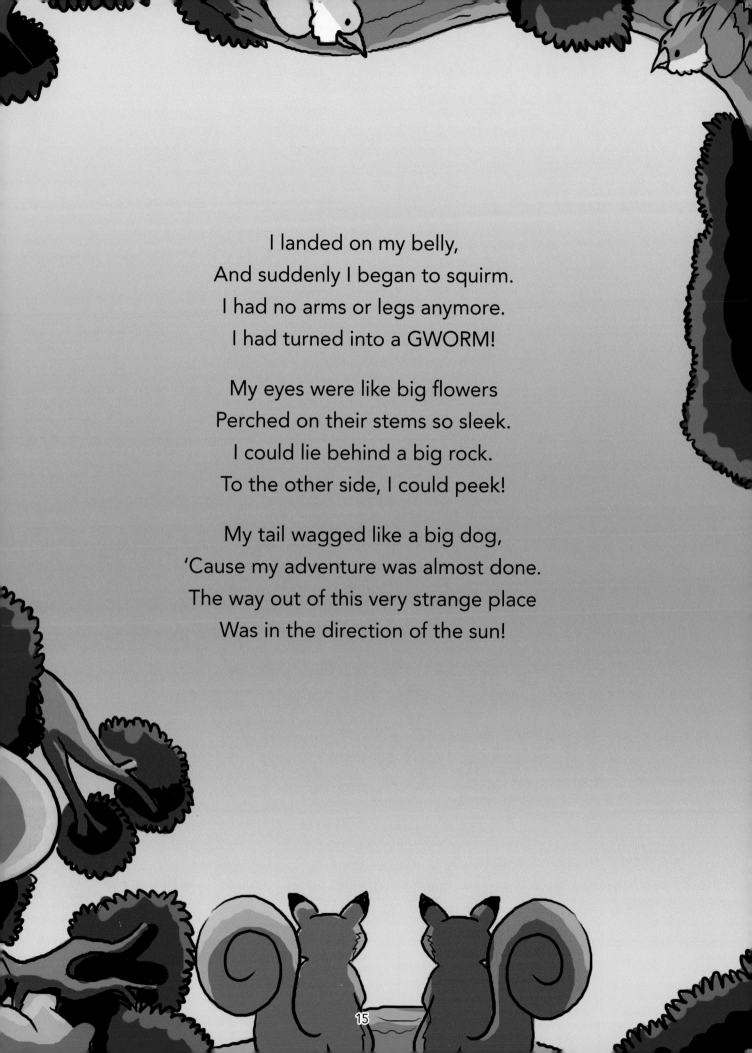

I landed on my belly,
And suddenly I began to squirm.
I had no arms or legs anymore.
I had turned into a GWORM!

My eyes were like big flowers
Perched on their stems so sleek.
I could lie behind a big rock.
To the other side, I could peek!

My tail wagged like a big dog,
'Cause my adventure was almost done.
The way out of this very strange place
Was in the direction of the sun!

And coming out of that forest,
I became the best-looking one you'll see!
Because everything turned to normal,
And I began to look like me!

The Ever-Changing Waters

After that last unusual adventure,
I thought to swim, I'd like to go.
I went out to a big blue lake
And jumped way down below.

I thought everything would be normal,
And I would have a lot of fun.
But then something unusual happened
Because a big change had just begun!

My hands turned into paddles,
And my feet became a fin.
My back had two large yellow humps,
Which made the fish turn around and grin!?

Again, everything was a'changing,
As I wasn't the same as before.
I had turned into a great, big KNISH,
And I wasn't sure if I wanted more!

So I swam down to the bottom,
Looking for a place to hide.
But that really didn't help that much
Because I noticed I had fins on my side!

And under those fins were eight legs,
And at the end of each was a knob.
I had turned to the color of a rainbow,
Because I was now an OCTOSLOB!!

My head was a big triangle,
And I had a big bubble for a nose.
And all along my furry body,
All my hair was found in rows.

So I left from that deep bottom.
To the fish, I gave a wave.
I swam toward that great, big opening,
Which turned out to be a cave.

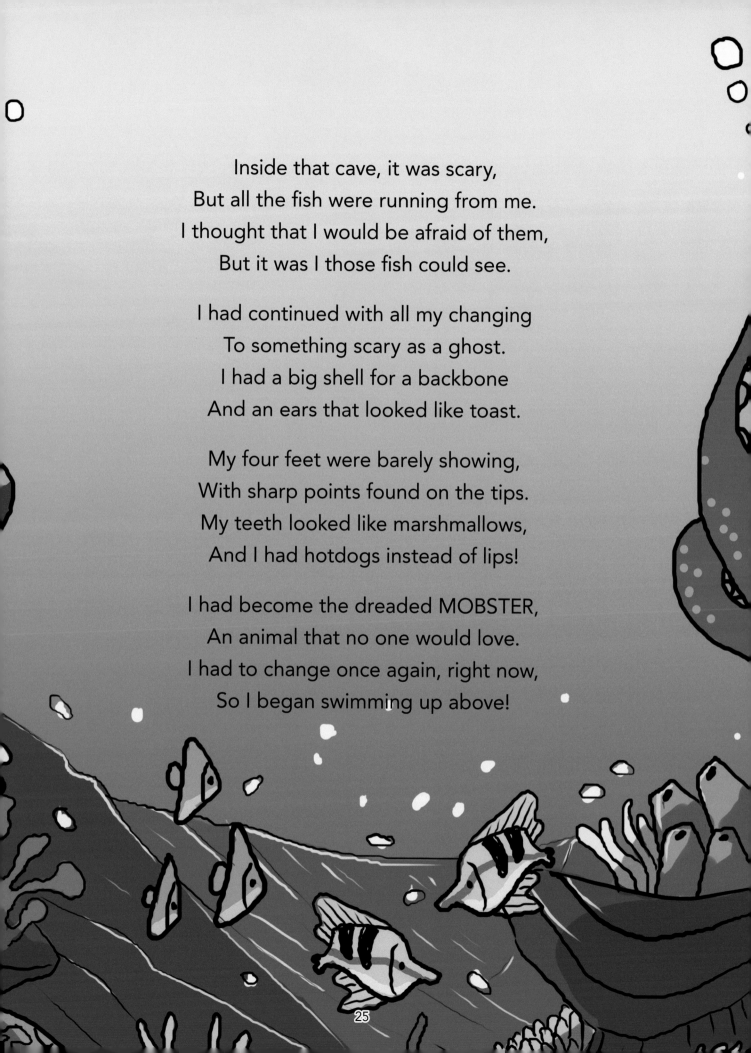

Inside that cave, it was scary,
But all the fish were running from me.
I thought that I would be afraid of them,
But it was I those fish could see.

I had continued with all my changing
To something scary as a ghost.
I had a big shell for a backbone
And an ears that looked like toast.

My four feet were barely showing,
With sharp points found on the tips.
My teeth looked like marshmallows,
And I had hotdogs instead of lips!

I had become the dreaded MOBSTER,
An animal that no one would love.
I had to change once again, right now,
So I began swimming up above!

And when I reached the surface,
I found a leaf where I could stop.
Then suddenly I got the strangest urge
That I could really hop and hop!

I noticed something quickly,
That my legs were slim and green.
And my tongue was blue and sticky
And was the longest you'd ever seen!

But that was part of being a BLOG,
A creature that could jump so high
That sometimes he would disappear
Way up in the big, blue sky.

I didn't want that to happen,
So into the water, I jumped once more.
I knew that this would change me again,
As it had several times before.

Once again into that water,
I landed with a splash.
Then suddenly I started itching
'Cause I had a yellow rash!

My skin had turned all prickly,
And my tail was full of goo.
And every time I took a breath,
I let out a loud and wet *achoo*!

And when I sneezed so briskly,
My body shook to and fro.
I was like a bowl of jelly
That didn't know where to go.

But I knew I had to go somewhere,
Because I didn't want to stay like I was.
I thought I'd go back where I jumped in
So I would stop being the dreaded GLUZ!

I looked for the place where I entered
This lake that was so blue.
To turn into another water beast,
I felt it just wouldn't do.

But it looked like I had no choice,
Because I changed into a star
With little paddles on each leg,
Which made me swim quite far.

So I swam around quite briskly
As a STARGLISH that moved so fast.
And then I looked right up ahead
'Cause the exit, I found at last!

I left the water quite quickly.
The change I knew was fate.
I was glad that I was back to "me,"
'Cause I knew "me" was always great!

The Ever-Changing Sky

After being all these strange creatures,
I thought I better just go back.
My parents would be looking for me,
And it was time to hit the sack.

And as I was a'running,
I could have sworn I was way up high.
Then I looked down toward my legs and feet
And noticed that I was in the sky!

My arms had turned into propellers,
And my body was like a boat.
And when I had to stop and rest,
I found that I could float!

Again, I knew it was happening,
Those adventures that were weird.
I was now up in the wide-open sky
As a wild and strange young BWIRD!

So I headed to the nearest cloud
So that I could rest and think.
Then all of a sudden, I was very large,
And through that cloud, I started to sink!

I had turned into a big fat GLOMB,
Since fat is the way that they are.
I had to flap my tiny wings,
Or I would fall to the ground so far.

I had a nose like a weather vane,
Which told me which way to go.
I knew I wanted to be something else,
So I just flew down very low.

At that point, I thought to rest awhile,
So I landed next to a hen.
I let out a cock-a-doodle-doo
As I started to change again.

My hair just started growing
And turned to a shade of white.
My body was skinny and the color of blue,
And I started to get some height.

I continued to grow up toward the sky.
I became bigger than ever before.
I was growing to be a GROOSTER,
And a cock-a-doodle-doo came out once more.

And when I was as tall as a house,
My legs started springing toward me.
My body acted like a slingshot,
And I shot so high you couldn't see.

And when I came to a stop so high,
I was scared I would fall to the ground.
Then a little parachute came out of my head,
And I landed, safe and sound!

And as I started walking along,
I just knew a change would happen.
My body became very plump and hard,
And my big, yellow wings started a'flappin'!

My face was like a beagle dog
With a tail like a purple snake.
This new form was the weirdest one,
And I was scared, for goodness' sake!

But when I opened my mouth to scream,
I was surprised that a squeak came out.
And every time I tried to speak,
A squeal was all I could shout!

I suddenly understood just what I was.
Yes, I had turned into a PICADEE.
I thought I had better change quite fast
Since the bigger birds could just eat me!

So I flew on toward a place I know
As the change was beginning to start.
I kept on flying back toward my home,
As this was the place that was in my heart.

But as I was up in the air so high,
Aiming toward the home I know,
My body became this bony thing,
And I rattled to and fro.

And at the end of my body,
I saw that my tail was like a rock.
I had become the fat old POSTRICH,
Who could only stand or walk!

This wasn't fun, so I started to jump
To see if a change would only occur.
Then I suddenly took off with a very loud shout,
As my body was covered with fur.

And as I flew toward my neighborhood,
I noticed that I was about to land
On a house, which was my very own,
And my dad gave me a hand.

He had seen that I was a flying QUARROW,
And he wasn't sure what he should do.
So he decided to grab me as I came down
And hold me till I was just like new.

So there I was in his loving grip,
And then I felt the change once more.
I wasn't sure what I had become,
But Dad let me in the door!

And on my way to my bedroom,
I passed a mirror that revealed to me
That I was back to my normal self again,
Which is who I should always be!

Printed in the United States
by Baker & Taylor Publisher Services